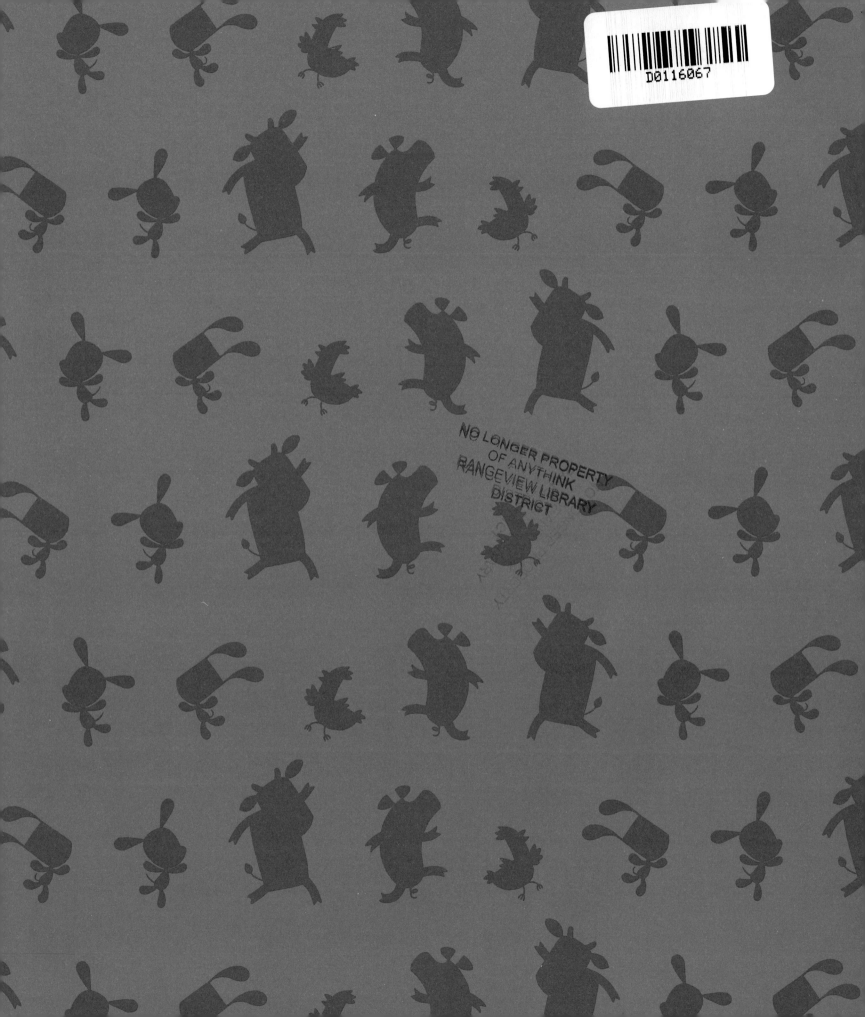

For my mum. You always told me "to keep on trying."
At least, that's what I thought you said. . . .

• First U.S. edition 2013 • Library of Congress Catalog Card Number 2012947824 • ISBN 978-0-7636-6616-3 • This book was typeset in Imperfect Bold, Cooper Five Opti Black, Countryhouse, Goudy Stout, and Kosmic. • The illustrations were done in pencil and digitally colored. • Candlewick Press, 99 Dover Sreet, Somerville, Massachusetts 02144 • visit us at www.candlewick.com
Printed in Heshan, Guangdong, China
13 14 15 16 17 18 LEO 10 9 8 7 6 5 4 3 2 1

STICK!

Andy Pritchett

CANDLEWICK PRESS

Worm!

CLUNK!